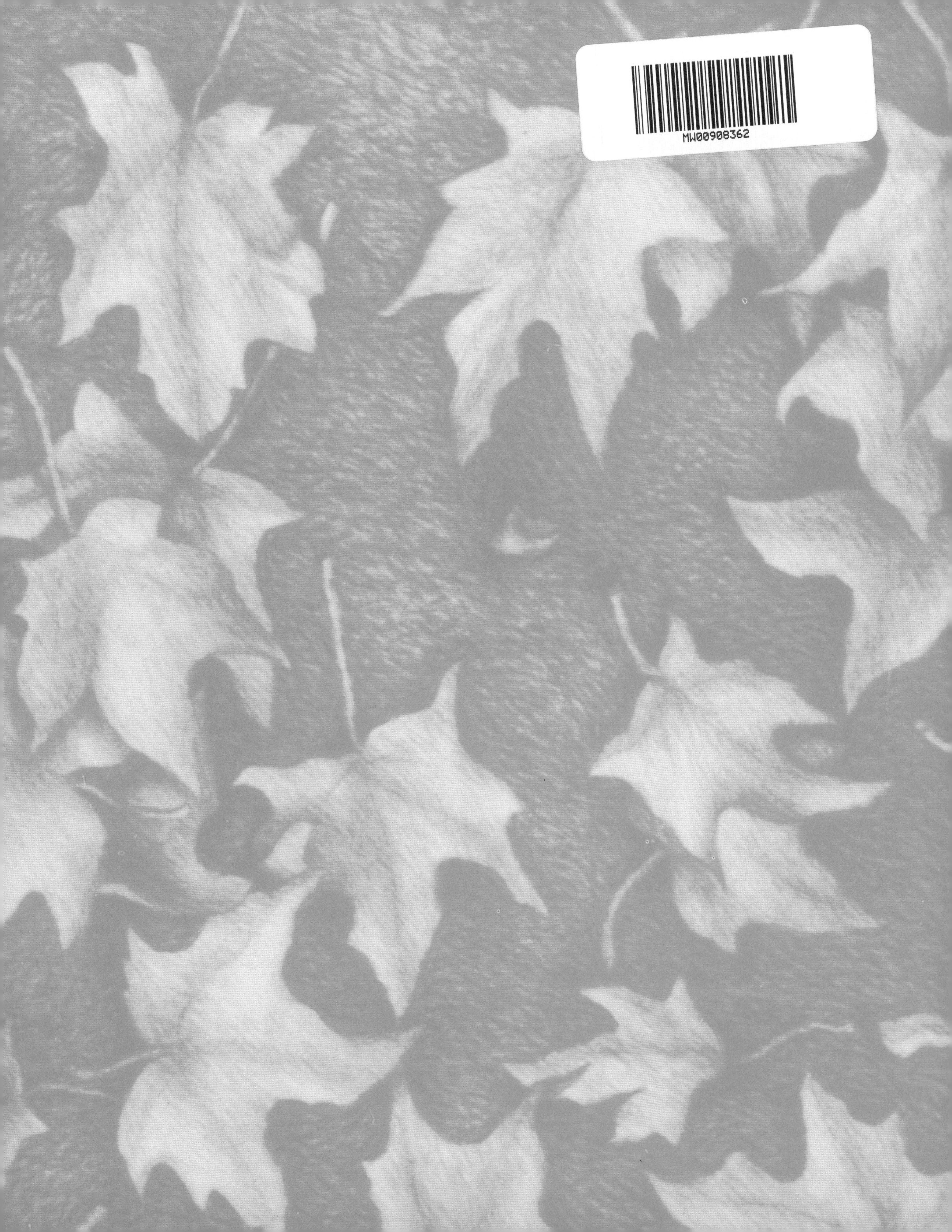

THE BOY
IN THE ATTIC

PAUL YEE

PICTURES BY
GU XIONG

A GROUNDWOOD BOOK

DOUGLAS & McINTYRE ✦ VANCOUVER TORONTO BUFFALO

ONE spring morning in China, Kai-ming Wong and his parents pulled on their best clothes and trekked to the nearby hills. They wanted to pay final respects at the tomb of Great-great-grandfather before boarding a bus to leave the village forever. Their destination? A city in North America full of glass towers and steel skyscrapers. Already the Wongs had given away their pots, blankets and few sticks of furniture.

Seven-year-old Kai-ming had never seen the tombs. For many years, traditional rituals had been banned throughout the country.

"Waste of money," thundered newspaper headlines.

"Foolish superstitions," blared the radio.

"Poor use of good land," shouted colorful posters.

Instead, the hills of tombs were transformed into plantations for peanut bushes.

When they reached the top, Kai-ming's parents looked at the mounded tombs and then at each other. Neither could remember the exact spot. Even though Ba and Ma used hoes to hack at the hard ground, soil and coarse grasses covered the headstones that remained.

"I'm certain it's one of these two." Ba wiped the sweat from his brow. "Such a long time since we've come up here."

"But which is the right one?" wondered Ma. She had spent an entire day cooking special dumplings. "We should do this properly."

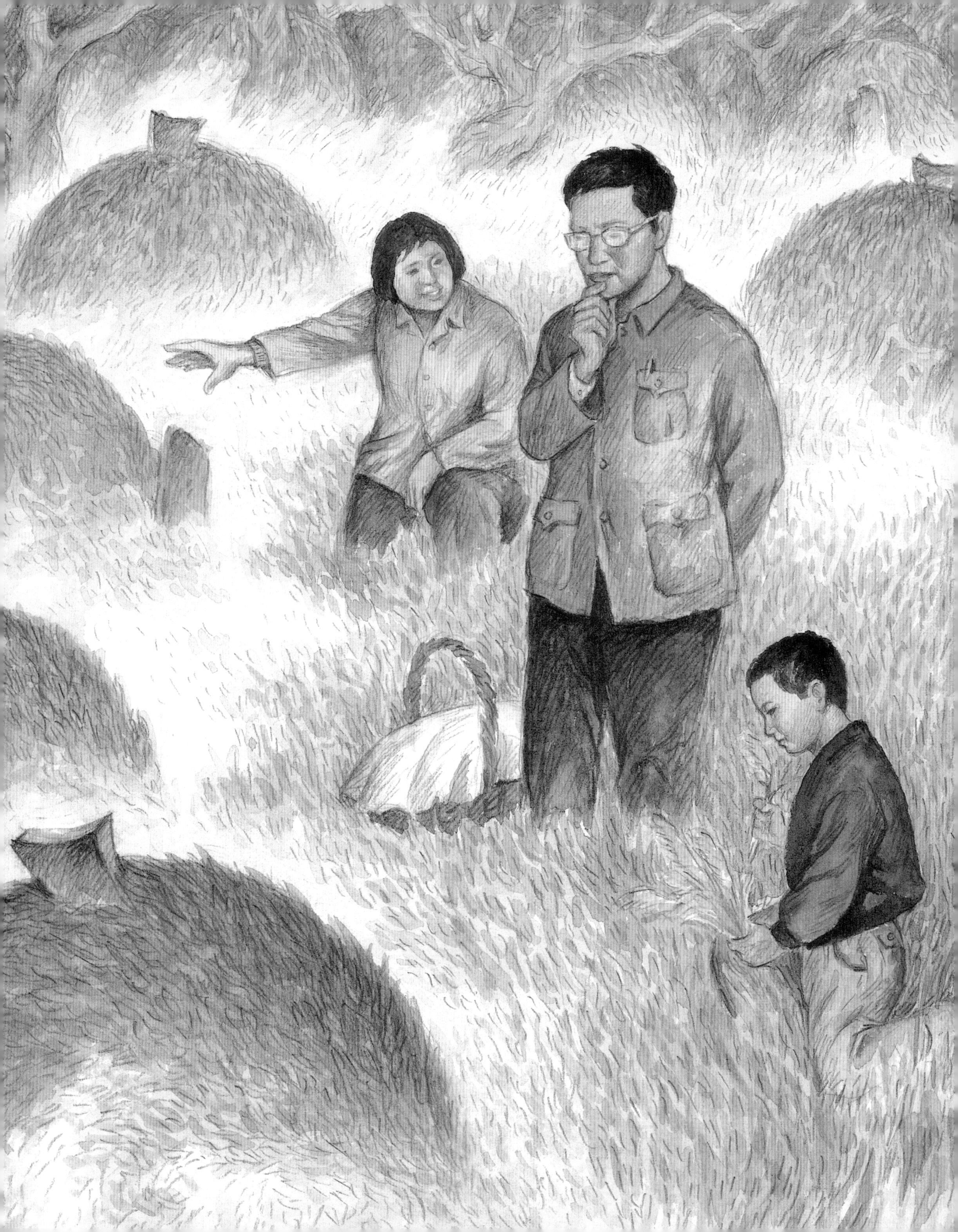

Kai-ming followed his parents from one mound to another. Suddenly Ma pointed at him. "Look!"

A black butterfly had landed on his arm. Never before had one flown so close.

"That must be it!" Ba hurried to the tomb beside his son. "The spirits have sent us a sign!"

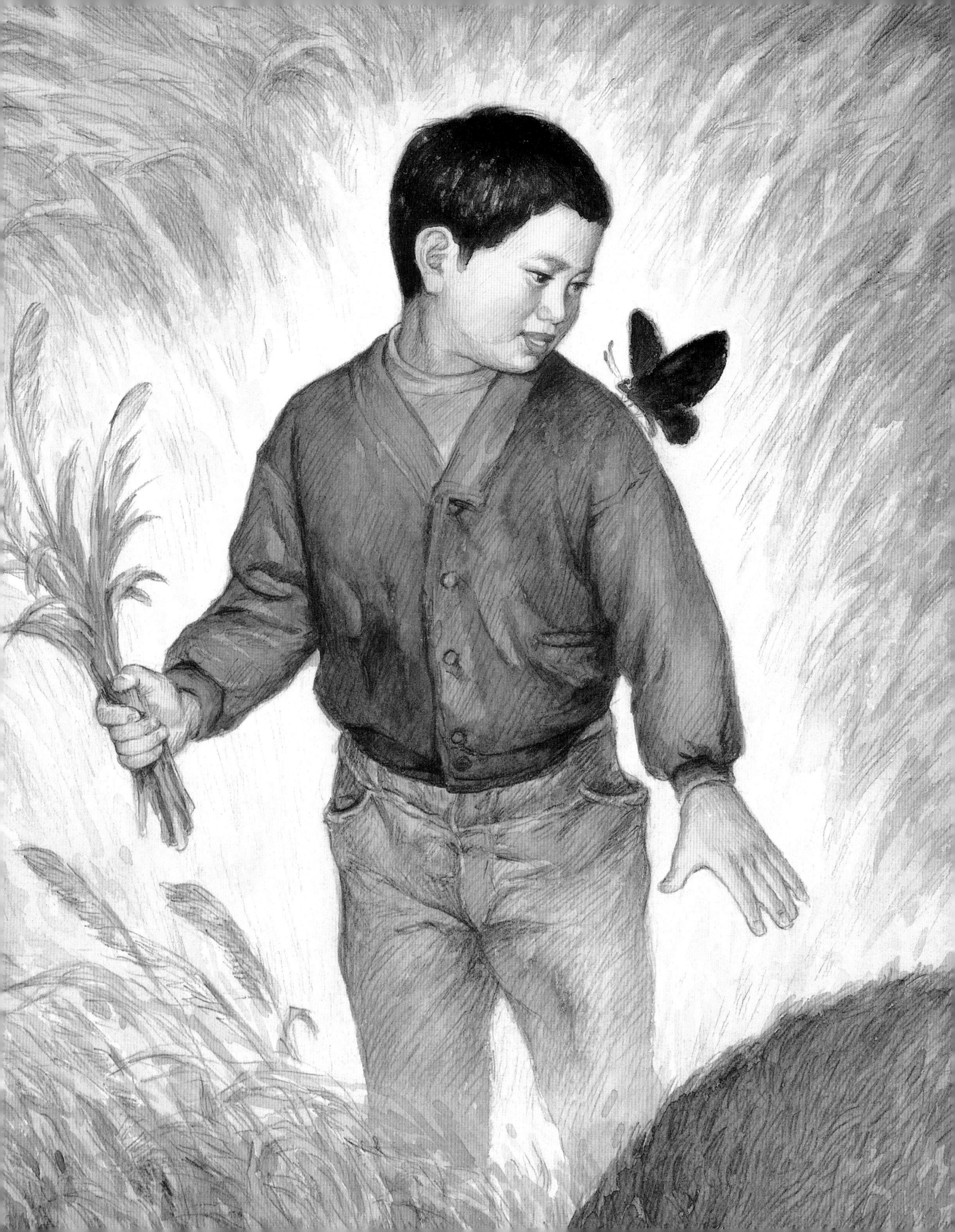

Ma lit incense, set out chopsticks and food, and burned some fake money, sending long wisps of smoke into the other world. Afterward, the family lingered a while, feeling very small as they gazed over the countryside they would never see again.

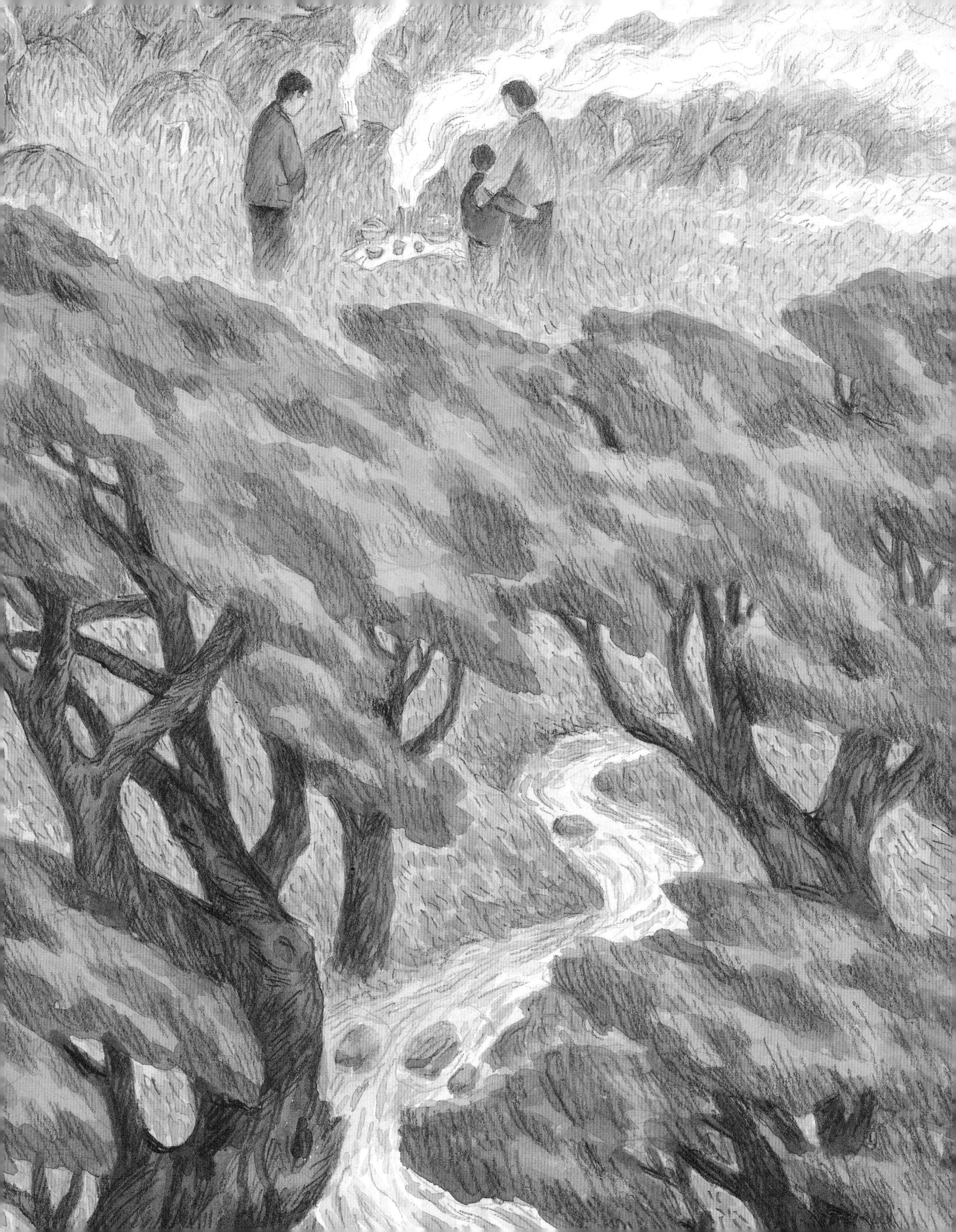

After the Wongs arrived in the big city, they rented an old house. Every day the parents went looking for work. Kai-ming stayed home, waiting for school to start in the autumn. For now, it was so warm and sunny he couldn't stay inside. But when he ventured out, he always returned quickly. Shiny cars and monster trucks sped by, and all along the road were windows and signs screaming strange words. Some might warn of danger, others might point to candy. But which was which? Children played hockey nearby, but he couldn't understand a single syllable of their shouting.

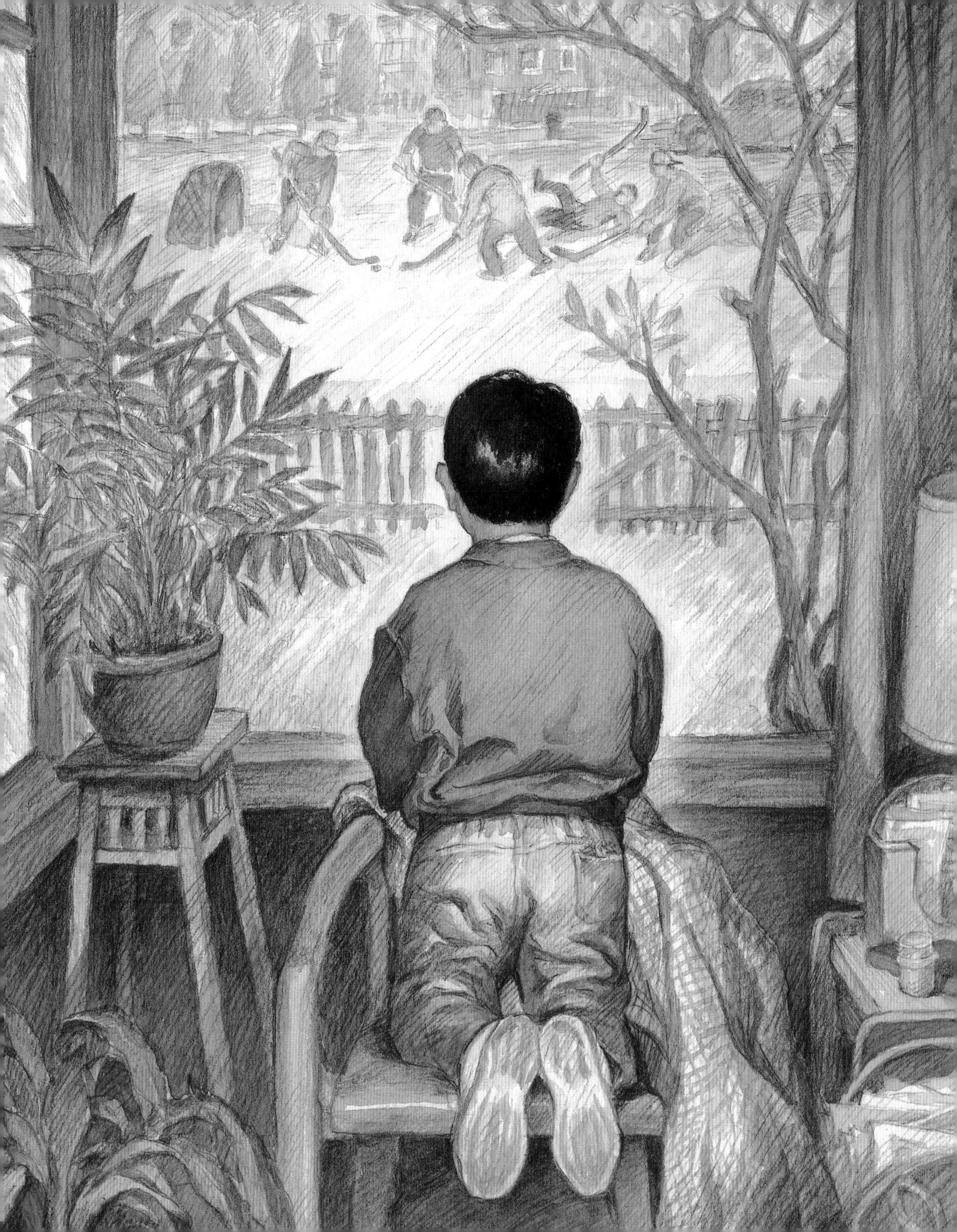

Behind the house lay a yard surrounded by a high picket fence, overgrown with weeds and shaded by a huge maple tree. The tree trunk was so thick that Kai-ming's arms couldn't reach around to climb. It stood so tall that he couldn't see the top, even though the chirping of newborn birds and squirrels' rustling could be heard among the leaves. In the afternoon, a canopy of green shaded the house and prevented the rooms inside from heating up too much.

Kai-ming stayed on the ground, pretending to be a hunter crawling through a dark, deep jungle, tracking wild animals with imaginary weapons. He had no toys, but Ba had promised to buy some soon.

One day he glanced toward the chimney and was startled. A human face was pressed to the attic window. But Ma had told him no one lived there.

Kai-ming ran up the stairs and found one door at the top, firmly locked. He figured his eyes had tricked him.

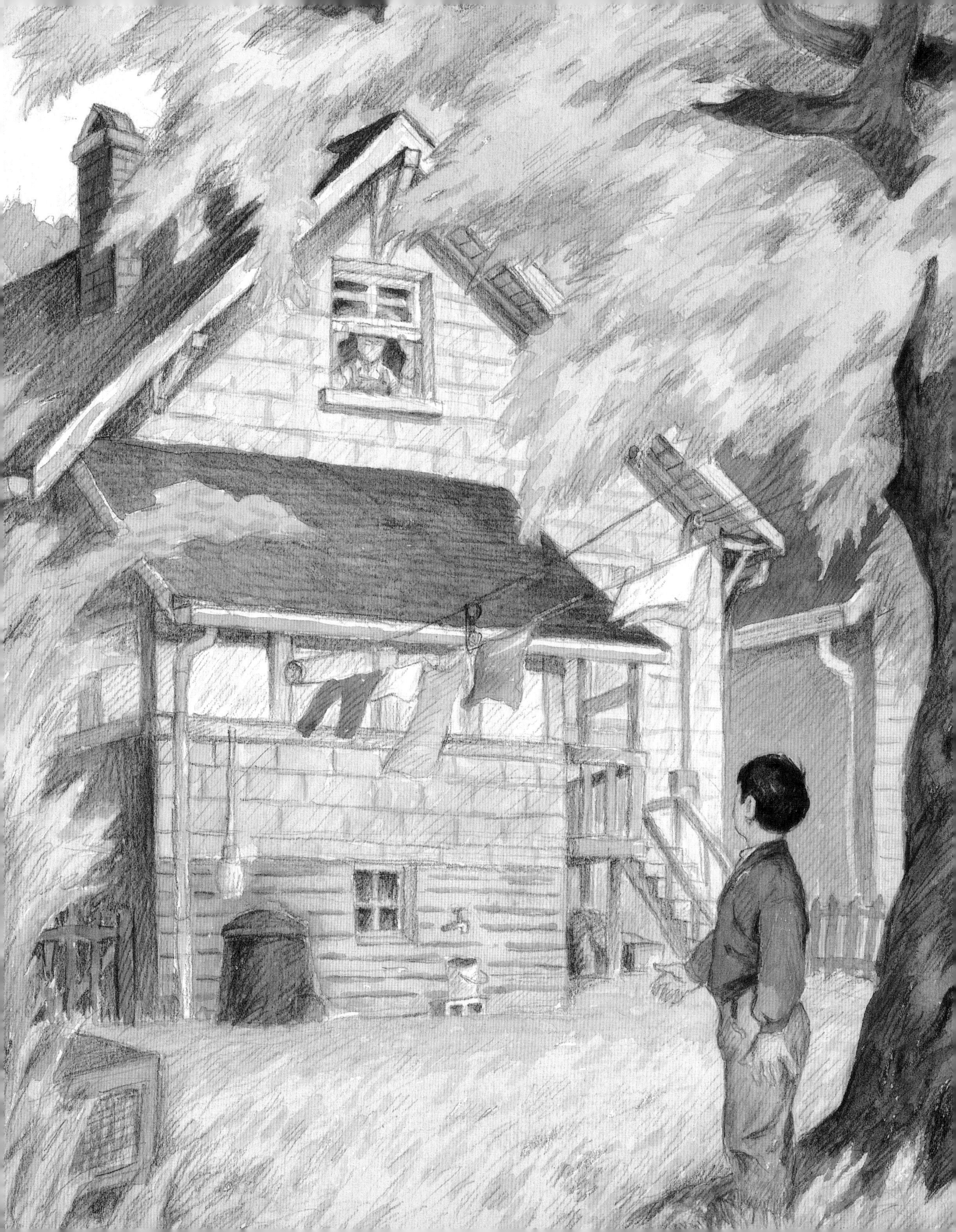

A few days later when Kai-ming looked toward the chimney, the face appeared again. He blinked, and still it stayed.

At the top of the stairs, he knocked loudly. No one answered. But when he turned the metal knob, this time the door opened.

The room yawned big and bright, with windows back and front. Dust particles danced happily on the beams of sunlight piercing the attic. In one corner stood a rusty trunk and a stack of ancient boxes. Through the windows, Kai-ming saw fast-moving street games, neatly tended backyards and the great maple tree. But no one was in the room.

When the weekend arrived, Ba and Ma took Kai-ming shopping and then to the park. He stayed close to them at all times. Having never ridden a subway train, Kai-ming stood in the front car and watched the silvery tracks rise up from the dark tunnel ahead and then disappear under him. Having never seen a wading pool, he wouldn't step into the water where children splashed and chased each other.

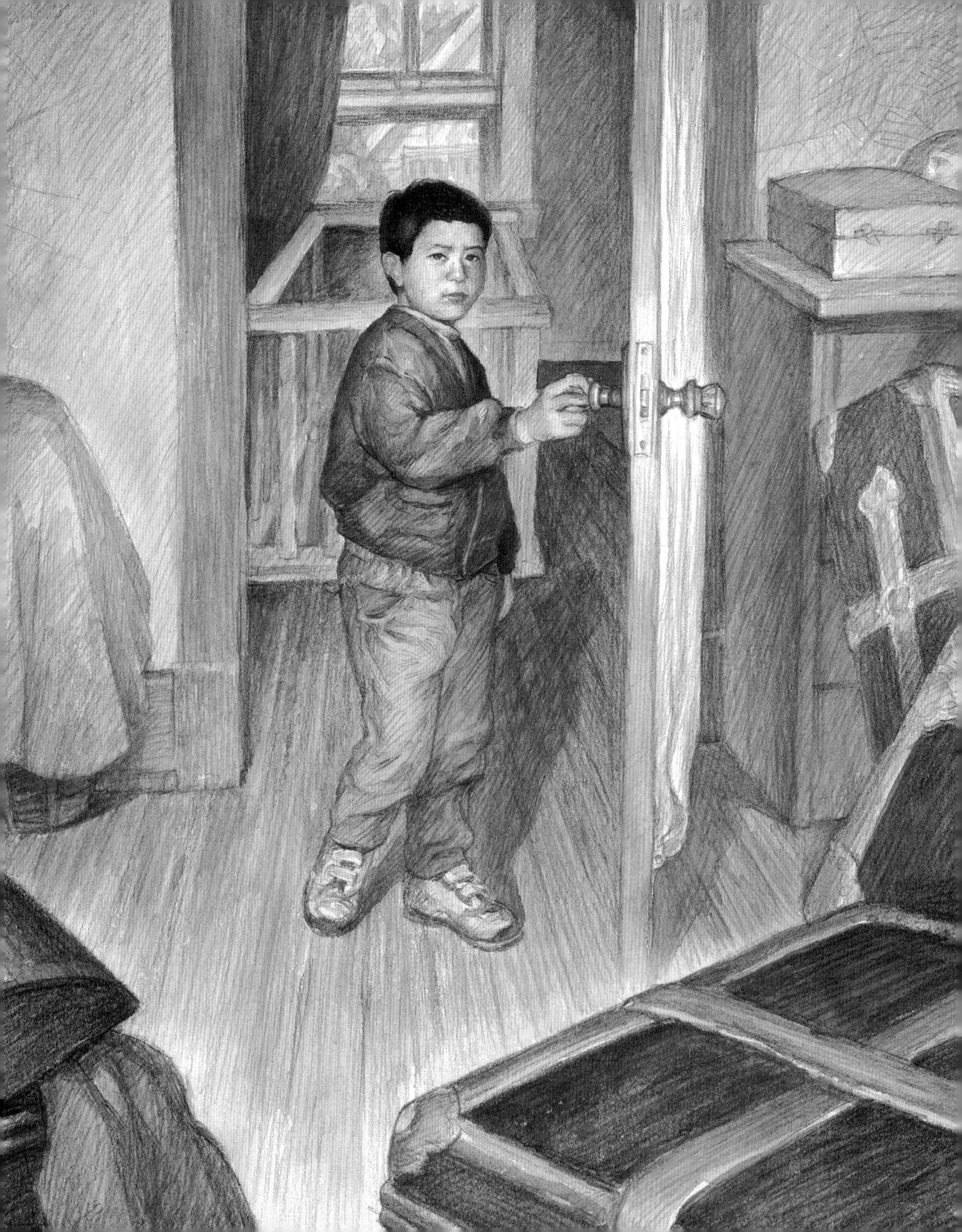

Days later, Kai-ming carried his lunch to the backyard. Glancing up, he saw the face again. He swallowed his food, and when the face remained there, he ran up the stairs and turned the doorknob.

A boy about Kai-ming's age stood by the window. He had corn-yellow hair, eyes of blue porcelain and apple-red cheeks. Despite the summer heat, he wore thick pants, heavy boots, a long-sleeved shirt and suspenders. None of the boys playing outside dressed like this.

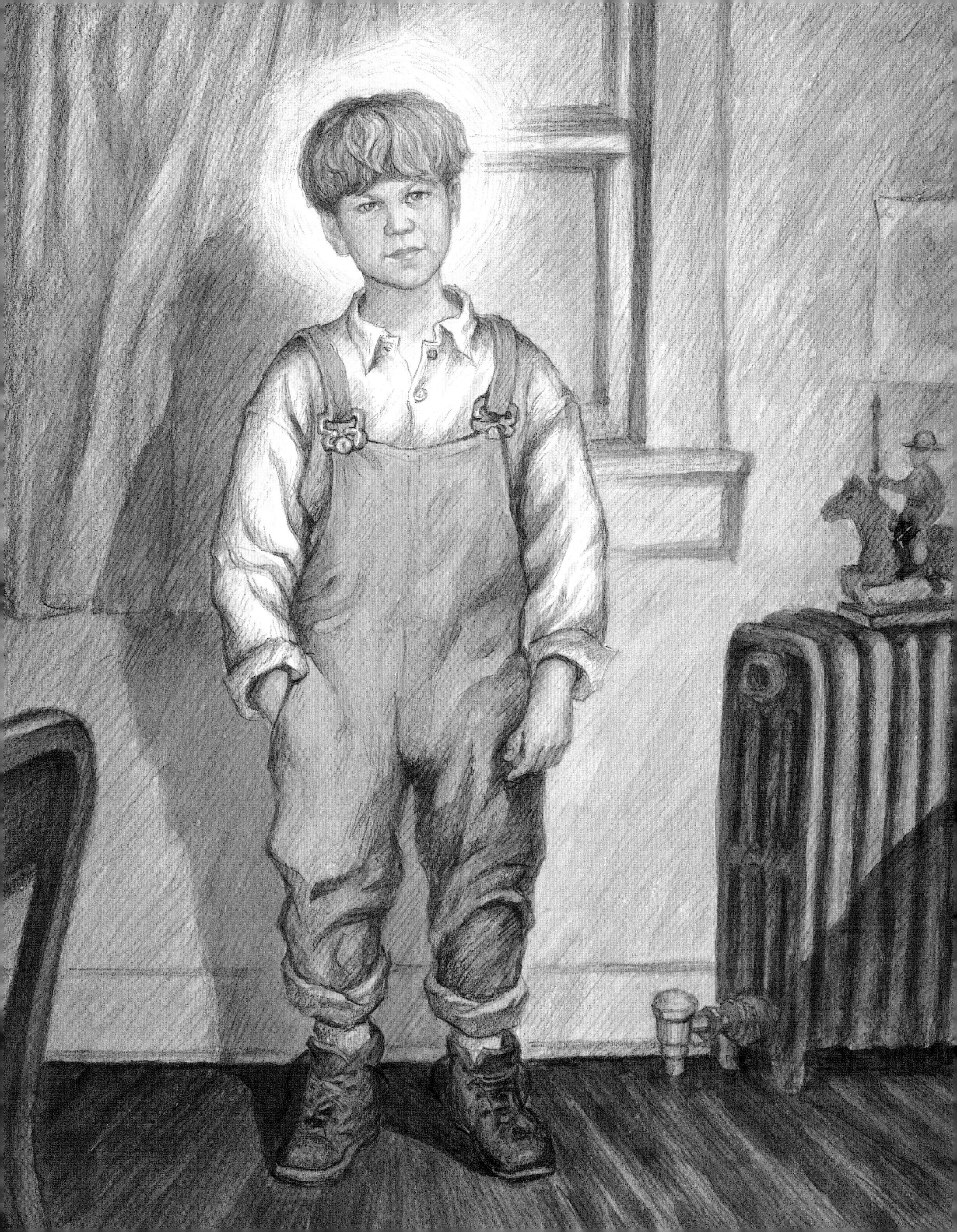

The boy called out, but his words were gibberish to Kai-ming. The sentences had rhythms and sounds he had never heard.

Shakily he replied, "Are you a ghost?"

The boy frowned. He didn't understand the Chinese words.

Kai-ming turned to the door but heard, "Wait, don't go."

He spun around and the boy was pointing at Kai-ming's shoulder. A black butterfly clung to him, close by his ear.

Slowly Kai-ming looked up. "You know my language?"

The boy shook his head. "No, but I understand you now. That must be a magic butterfly. Do you want to play?"

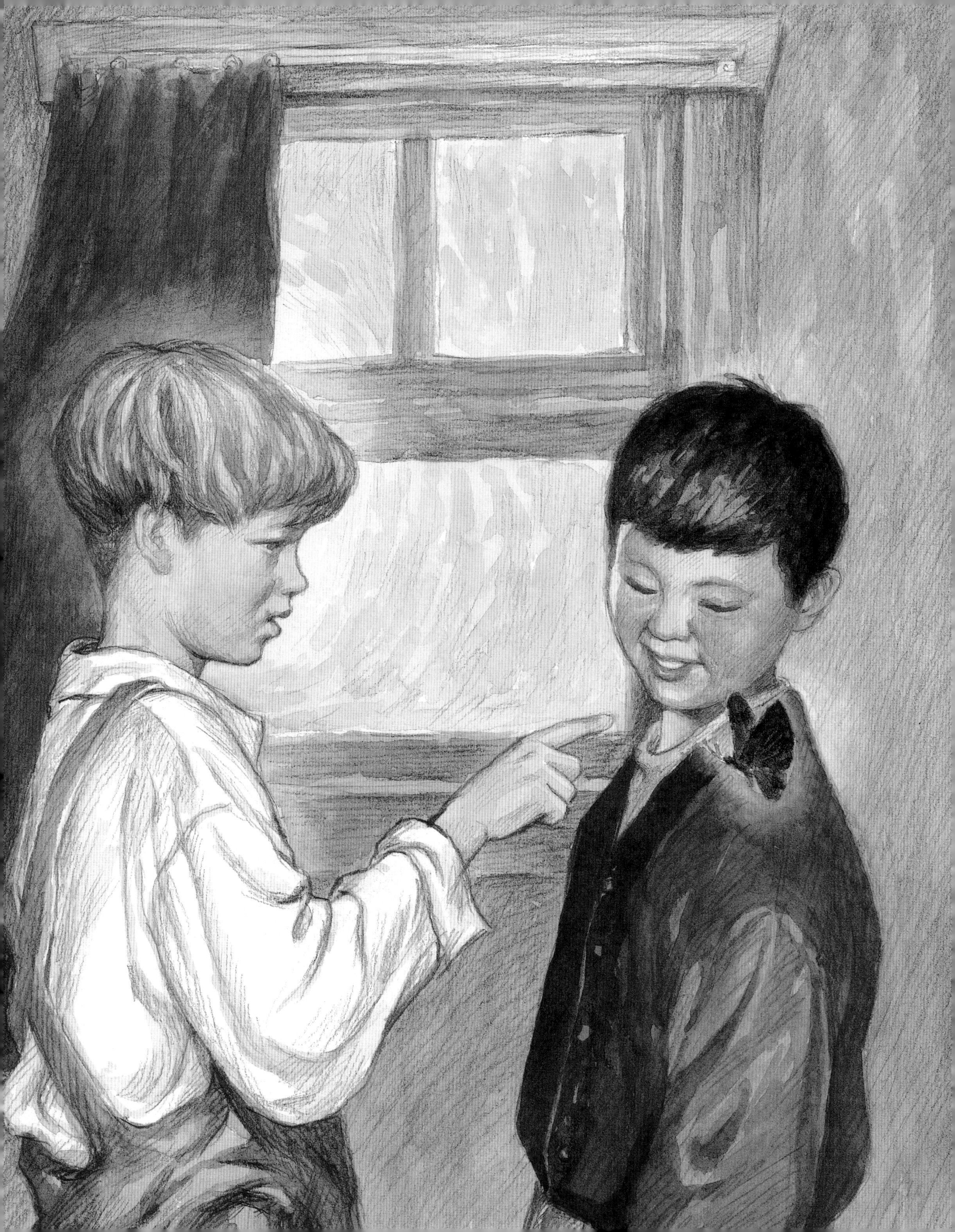

His name was Benjamin, and the trunk and boxes in the corner were filled with his toys.

Every day, when Ba and Ma went job-hunting, Kai-ming crept upstairs to play with his new friend. They shaped railway tracks into two circles criss-crossing the room and raced each other in opposing directions. When the hand-cranked top came spinning across the floor and derailed the cars, a battalion of wooden horses and soldiers galloped to the rescue.

"Choo-choo!" shouted Kai-ming.

"Clickety-clack, clickety-clack," cried Benjamin.

When masked bandits felled a tree across the tracks, the model train screeched to a stop, and the crew relinquished its money box and gold. The boys leapt onto the rocking horse to chase the robbers, shouting, "Giddyap! Go, boy, go!" Faster and faster they went, until the beast almost overturned.

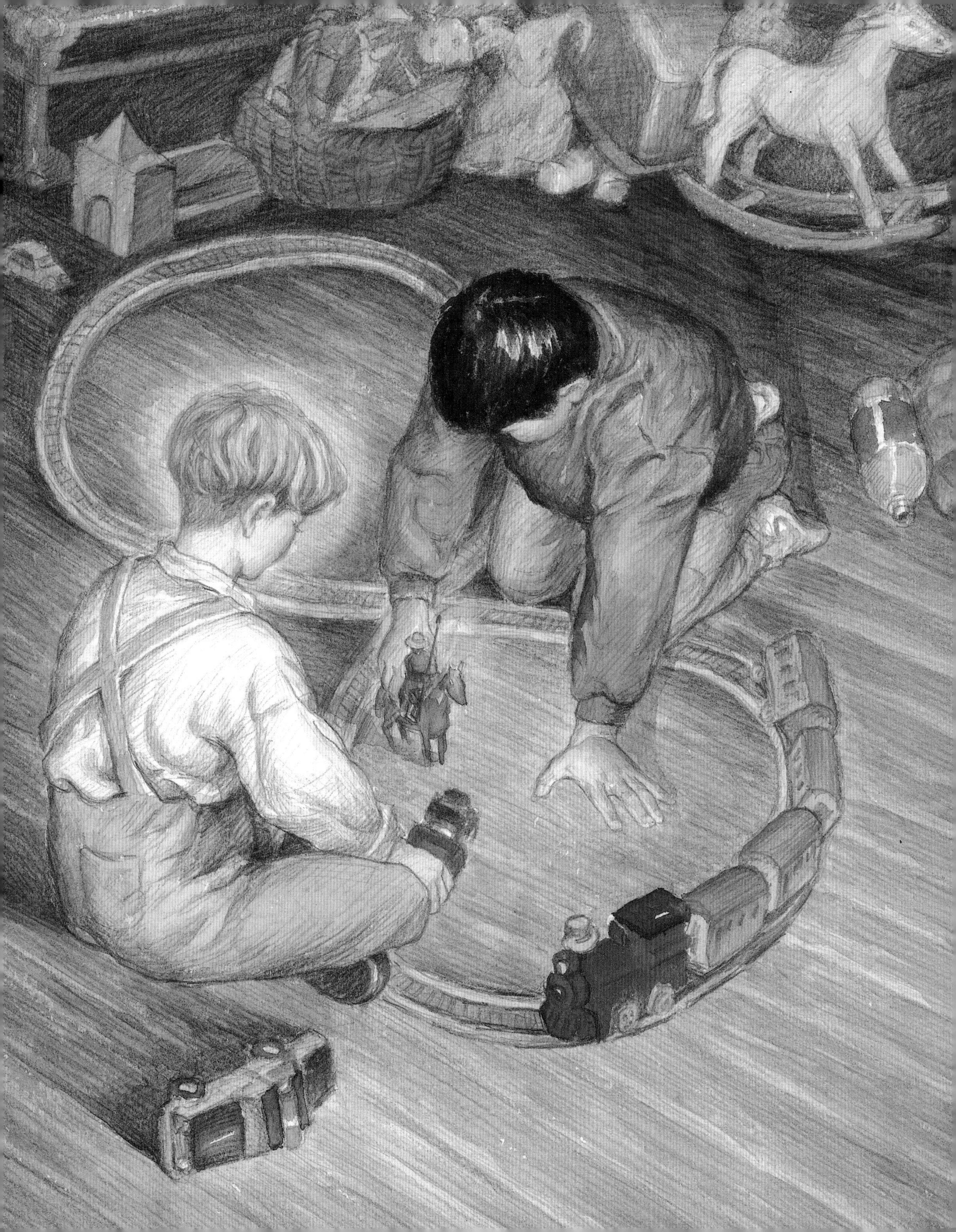

The summer days sped by as the boys laughed and chased away the afternoons. Kai-ming told no one about his special friend.

One day the boys sat cross-legged, and Benjamin told his story: "When my family moved into this house, it was just finished, so we could touch wet mortar and smell fresh-cut wood. One day I made my baby sister cry, so my mother locked me up here. Although I knew it was just for a little while, I decided to slide down the drainpipe and give her a scare. But I slipped and fell and broke my neck. In her grief, my mother brought all my toys up here and shut the door. Then they moved away and left all my things behind."

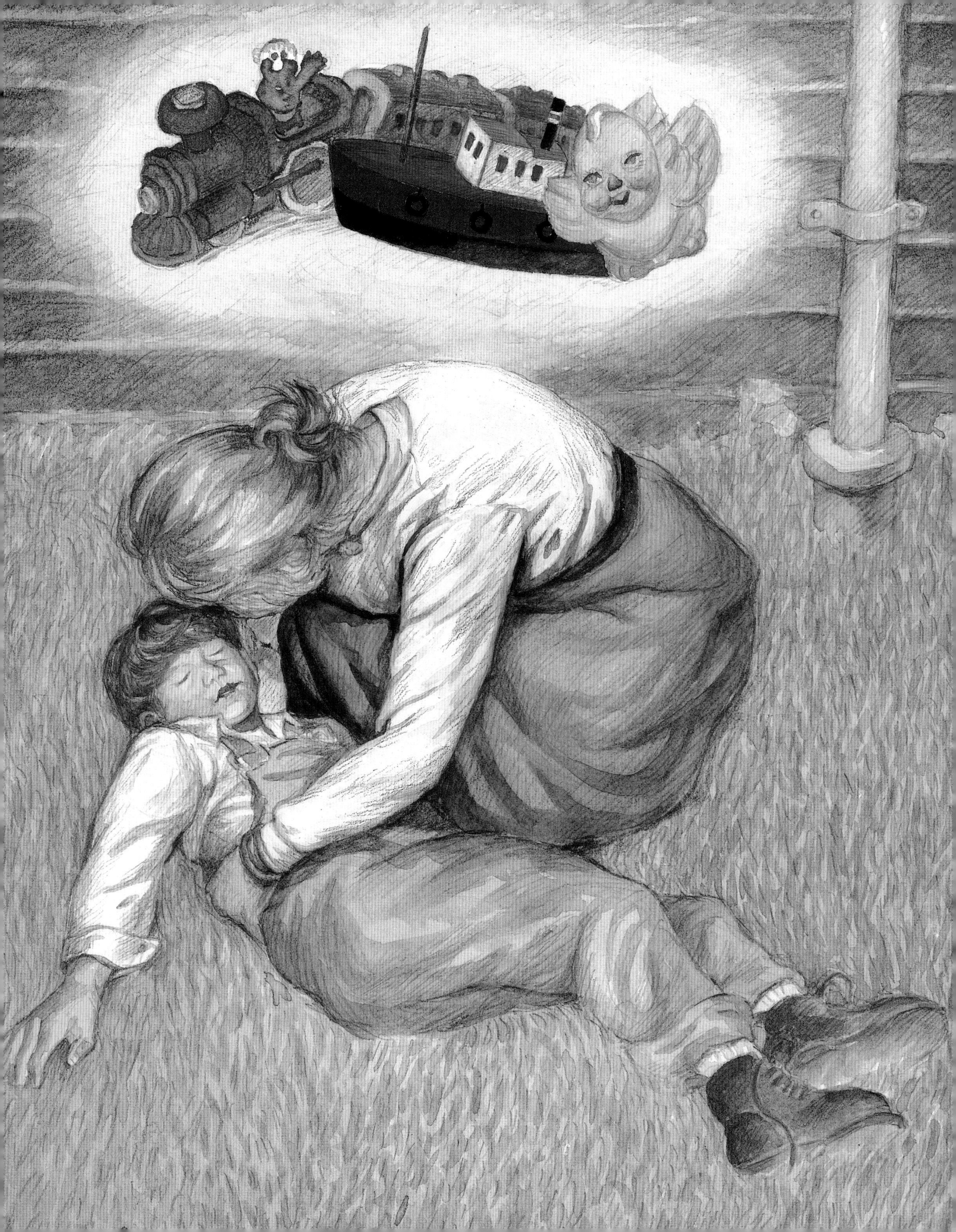

At dinner that night, Ba cleared his throat and smiled. "I've found a job and we can afford a newer house. So it's time to move."

"But I like it here," cried Kai-ming. "I don't want to leave."

Too bad. Ba had already made up his mind.

When Kai-ming went back to the third floor, he had a long face. As usual, the black butterfly appeared so the two boys could talk. "My father says we're moving."

His friend nodded. "I know."

"Will you come with me?"

Benjamin shook his head. "All my toys are here."

"Bring them along! The new house will have lots of room."

Still he wouldn't go.

"And there will be new toys," Kai-ming persisted. "If you come, we'll play together."

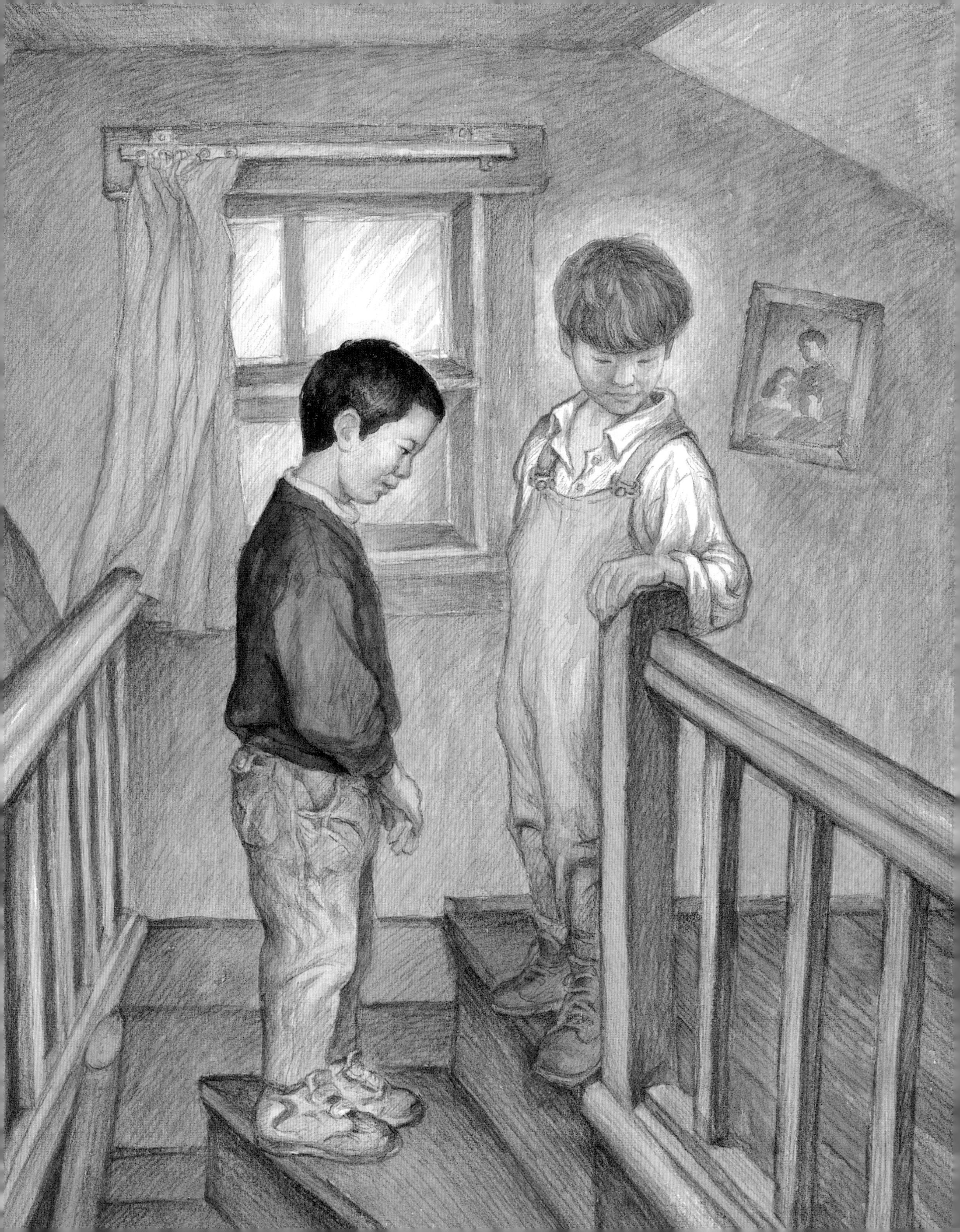

When the answer stayed the same, he slammed the door and ran downstairs. Ba had purchased a TV for the family and new games for his son. For a while, Kai-ming watched cartoons and commercials and shook the playthings from their boxes. But playing felt different than before.

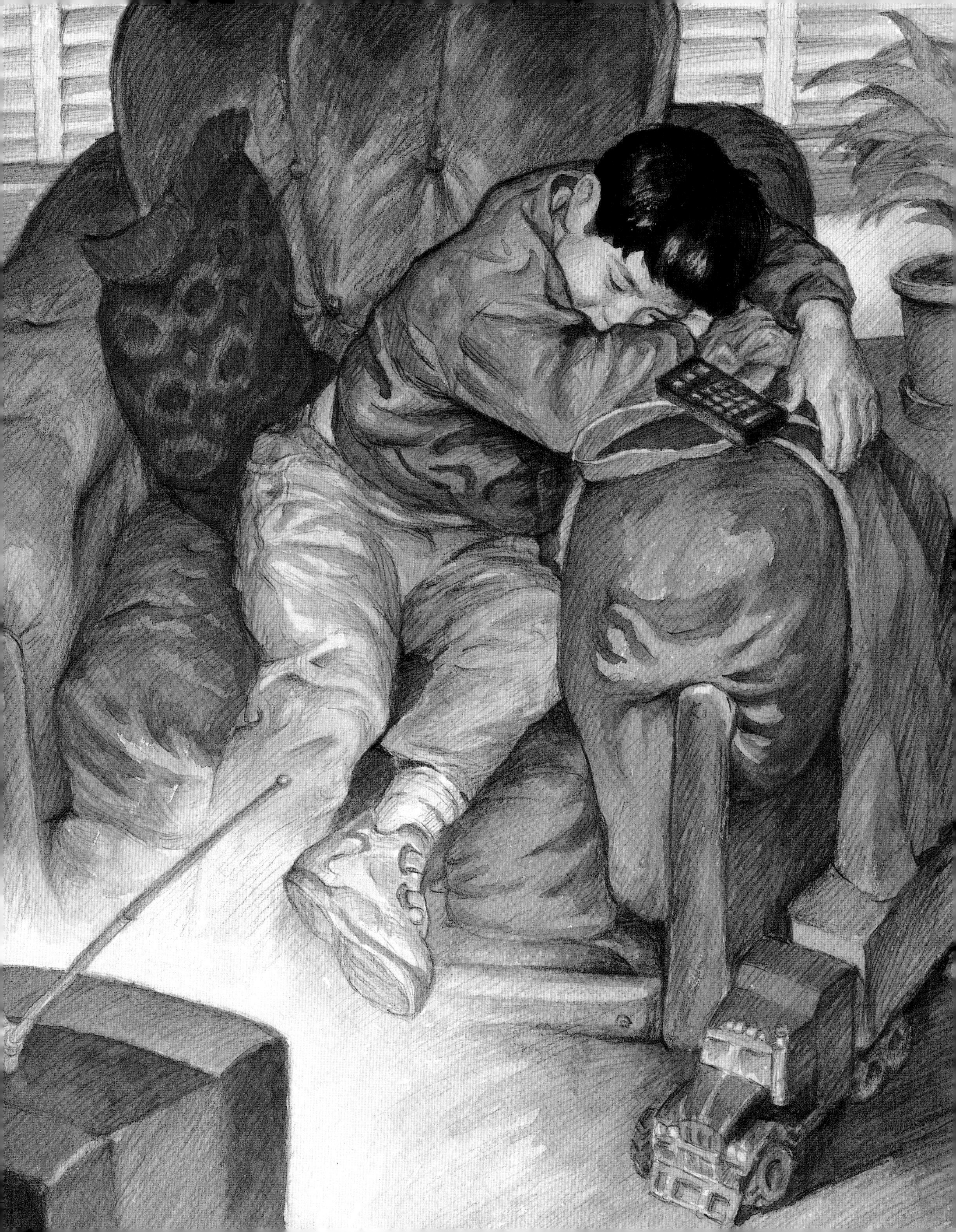

The day before the moving van came, Kai-ming shoved aside his plastic cars and battery-run games and ran upstairs. His friend was bent over a jigsaw puzzle and looked up grinning, as if nothing had changed.

"Ready to play?" he asked.

"No."

Benjamin shrugged and turned back to his pieces. Kai-ming stood and watched. Finally he said, "You like playing alone, don't you?"

The yellow-haired boy didn't move. "It's always more fun with other people."

Kai-ming stepped forward. "I want to play with you."

Blue eyes glared back. "You'll grow up and leave me behind."

"That's not true!" Kai-ming knelt. "You can come with me."

Benjamin shook his head. "I can't leave."

Kai-ming jumped to his feet. "You don't like me, do you? Isn't that the real reason you won't come?"

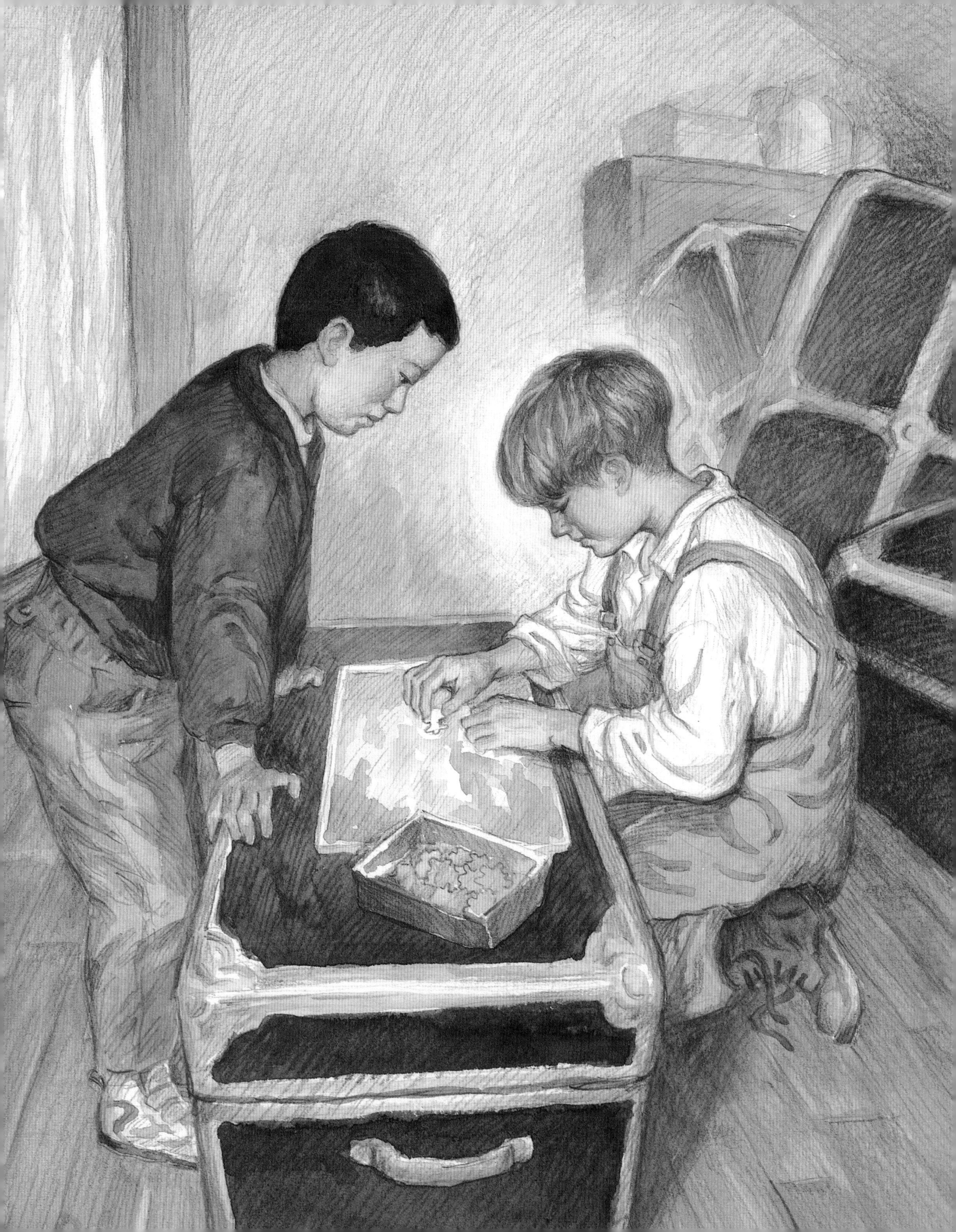

Benjamin sighed. Finally he walked to the window and pressed his nose to the glass. "See that tree? I've climbed to its top."

Even from the attic, the maple stretched high above them, its branches spread out wide and curved like the ribs of a grand umbrella.

Kai-ming shook his head. "You're lying! Nobody could go that high!"

Benjamin stared out over the shingles. "When that tree was young, it stood only a few feet high and all its branches dipped close to the ground. It was easy to swing my way up. Over the past eighty years, it has grown a hundred times taller. But I haven't added an inch to my height. Ghosts never grow older."

The tree loomed like a mountain with leafy curtains, thick as blankets. The birds had abandoned their nest and squirrels scampered about, storing food for winter. A few leaves had dried into yellow and red and fallen to the ground.

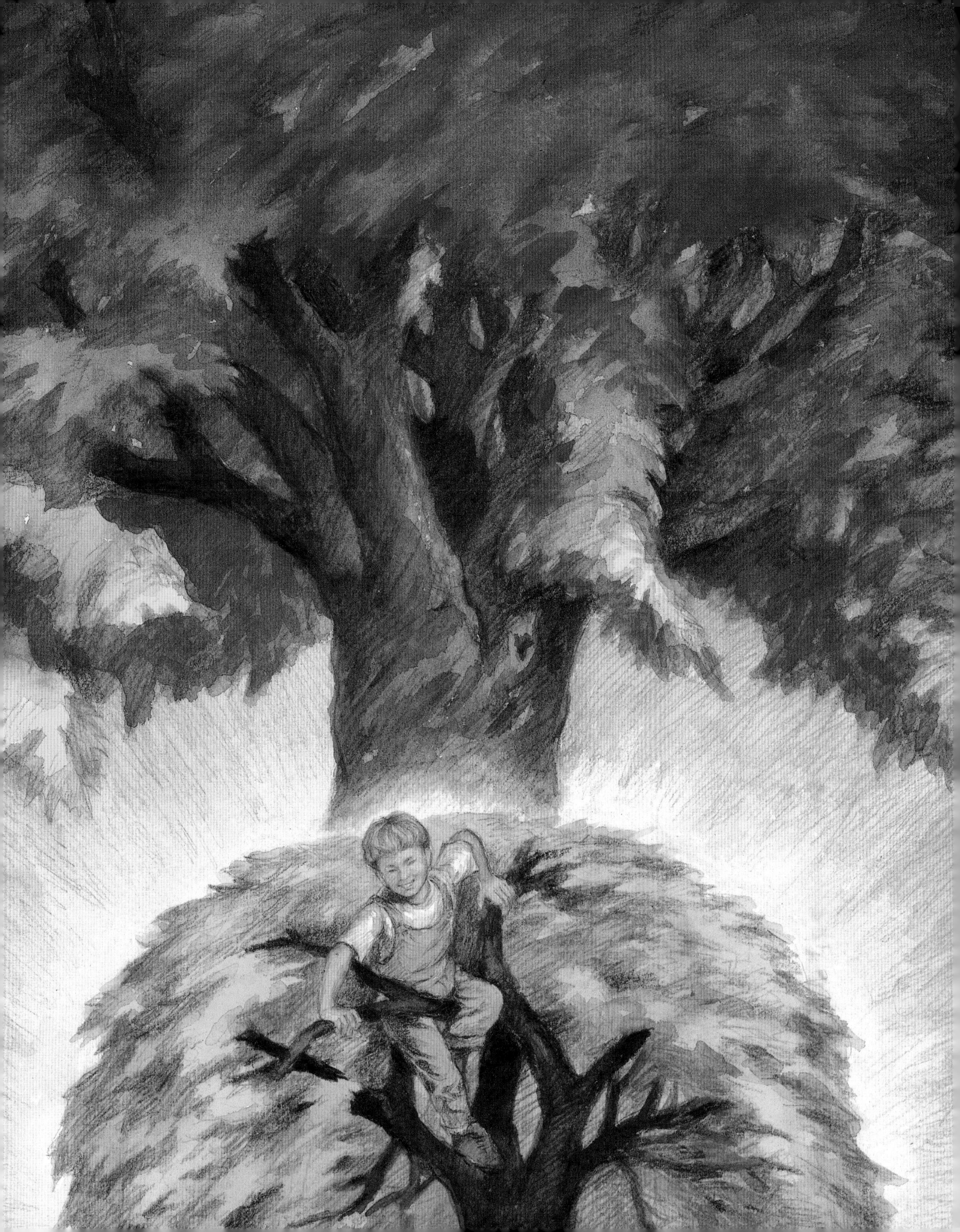

Now Kai-ming understood. Gently he lifted the black butterfly off his shoulder and onto Benjamin's. "Take this," he said. "No matter who comes here, you can talk freely. I'll be learning English soon."

The two boys smiled, shook hands and went separate ways. Kai-ming made many new buddies, but he never forgot his first friend in the big city.

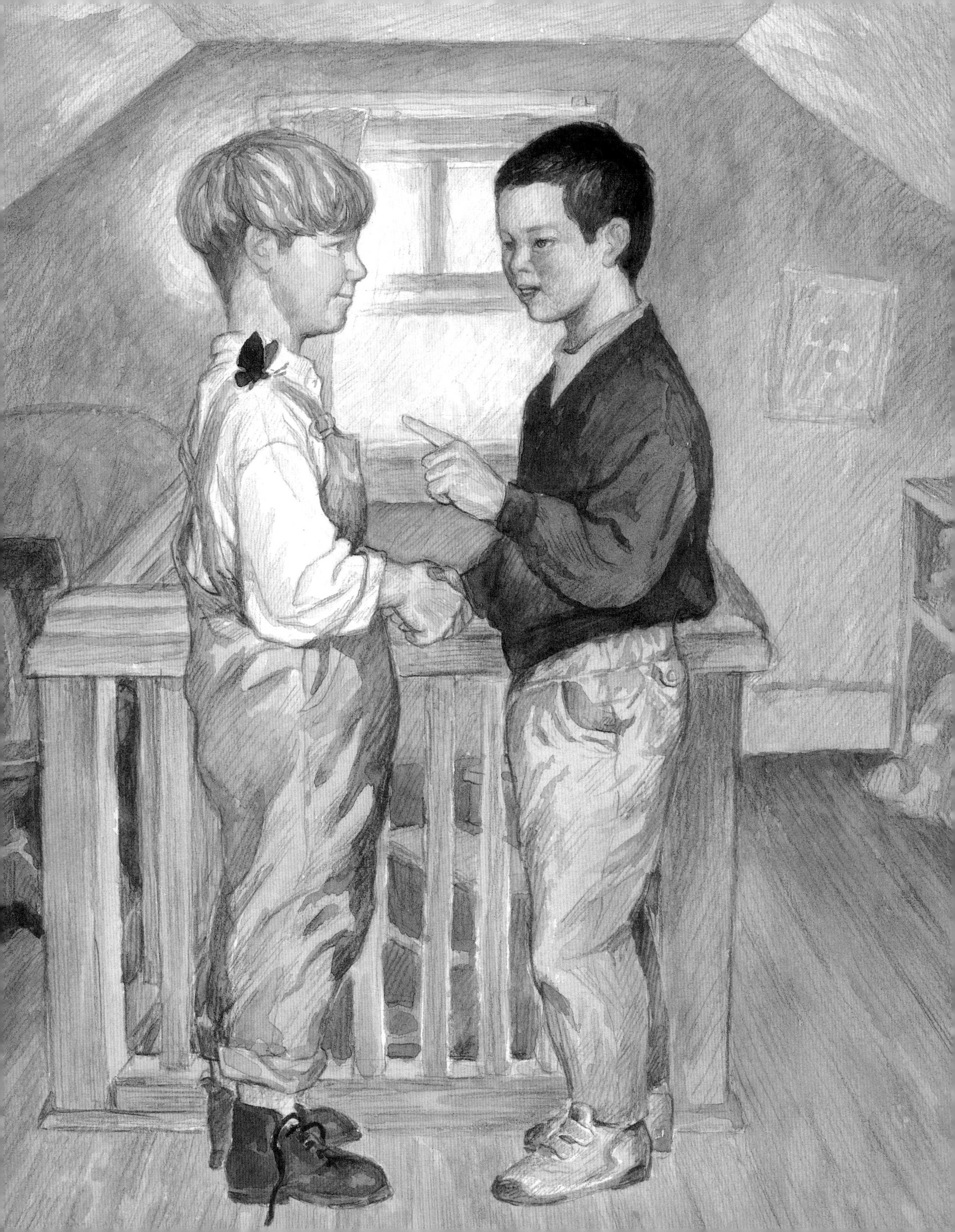

For Jonah Lev Lefkowitz

PY

To my wife Ge Ni and my daughter Gu Yu
With memories of moving to Vancouver from China

GX

𝒞

Groundwood Books / Douglas & McIntyre
585 Bloor Street West
Toronto, Ontario M6G 1K5

Distributed in the U.S.A. by
Publishers Group West
1700 Fourth Street
Berkeley, CA 94710

We acknowledge the financial assistance of the Canada Council
for the Arts, the Ontario Arts Council and the Government of
Canada through the Book Publishing Industry Development
Program for our publishing activities.

Library of Congress Data is available.

Canadian Cataloguing in Publication Data
Yee, Paul
The boy in the attic
"A Groundwood book".
ISBN 0-88899-330-7
I. Xiong, Gu, 1953- . II. Title.
PS8597.E3B69 1998   jC813'.54   C98-930992-4
PZ7.P38Bo 1998

Design by Michael Solomon
Printed and bound in China by Everbest Printing Co. Ltd.